Moving Time for Kelly

written by Phyllis Martin

illustrated by Susan Yoder

Library of Congress Catalog Card Number 87-91994
Copyright ©1988, Phyllis Martin
Published by The STANDARD PUBLISHING Company, Cincinnati, Ohio
Division of STANDEX INTERNATIONAL Corporation. Printed in U.S.A.

Once there was a very unhappy little
girl named Kelly. At least she thought she
was unhappy. But she wasn't really as
unhappy as she thought she was. She just
felt sad because her family had moved to
a new town. And Kelly was sure she was
the only little girl who ever had to move
away and leave her friends.

"Mother," she said, "I don't have any friends since we moved, do I?"

"Kelly, you have more friends now than ever before. One of your new friends is a big person. She's the woman who sold us this new house. Her name is Carla Miller.

"Not only is Mrs. Miller your friend but she has other friends your age who live near us. They want to be friends with you too. You'll meet two of them soon. They are Katie and Jeff."

"I don't want new friends," cried Kelly. "I want to keep my old friends."

"You can make new friends and keep your old friends too."

"How, Mother? How can I keep my old friends?"

"When you learn to write you can send cards to them. I'll send some cards for you right now. We'll tell your long-time friends where we live now, and I'll help you sign your name on the cards. Then, for your birthday we'll call them. That is, we'll call at least two of your old friends. You can choose the ones you want to call."

"But, Mother, this place seems so funny. And, I don't have toys or anything I had at home — my real home."

"Kelly, *this* is your real home now. And you do have toys. All your favorites are here. They're in those boxes. There's even a surprise packed somewhere in them — a teddy bear! You'll see him as soon as we unpack.

"And, do you remember those pretty red and yellow flowers that used to come up in the spring at our other house? Our tulips? Well, I brought along some bulbs from them to plant here. They'll bloom here just as they did before we moved."

"No, Mother, they'll be different. Everything's different here."

"Your cat Inky's not different. But he can tell — just as you can — that some things are different. But, Kelly, a lot is the same here.

"For one thing, the stars are the same. When things seem to change too fast for me, I look up in the sky at the unchanging stars. Then I feel safe and warm."

Kelly looked puzzled, so her mother told her more about the stars.

"You see, Kelly, stars form a map in the sky. God put them there to guide us. Because He made the North Star so bright, that's the one I always look for."

Kelly jumped up and down and almost shouted, "That's the one you showed me before, isn't it, Mother? Isn't it?"

"Yes, it is. And we can find it again tonight just as we did where we used to live.

"After we find it, I'll listen while you pray your new prayer to God. That's when you'll know that this is now your real home."

Help Kelly find the North Star.
Which star is it?

Later that night Kelly's mother
smiled as she looked at Kelly snuggled
between Inky and her new teddy bear.
She listened as Kelly prayed.